To Bella and her hurly-burly hullabaloo.
–T. A.

To my grandmother Märta, for all those summers spent enveloped in your world of art, books, and your dry sense of humor.
–Å. G.

 First published in 2021 by Page Street Kids, an imprint of Page Street Publishing Co., 27 Congress Street, Suite 105, Salem, MA 01970, www.pagestreetpublishing.com.
Distributed by Macmillan, sales in Canada by The Canadian Manda Group. ISBN-13: 978-1-64567-286-9. ISBN-10: 1-64567-286-7. CIP data for this book is available from the Library of Congress. This book was typeset in Mikado. The illustrations were created digitally with hand-drawn textures.
Cover and book design by Julia Tyler for Page Street Kids. Printed and bound in Shenzhen, Guangdong, China.
21 22 23 24 25 CCO 5 4 3 2 1

Page Street Publishing uses only materials from suppliers who are committed to responsible and sustainable forest management.
Page Street Publishing protects our planet by donating to nonprofits like The Trustees, which focuses on local land conservation.

Meena's Mindful Moment

Tina Athaide

illustrated by Åsa Gilland

PAGE STREET KIDS

When the mangoes are sweet and guava ripe,
Meena visits Dada.
And wherever Meena goes . . .

her hurly-burly hullabaloo goes too.

In the mornings, Dada takes Meena to greet the sun.
She stands like a flamingo and stretches her arms.

Dada sits cross-legged.
"Shhhh!"
Meena scowls.

She's a tree.
Just like Dada.

But then, her throat tickles with songs and
she doesn't know how to make it stop.

ZOOM!

Meena explodes, singing
and spinning like a hurricane.

And whatever Meena does, her hurly-burly hullabaloo does too.

Meena's days are busy and full.
She twirls and swirls,
sprinting in and around and upside down.
Dada shakes his head. "Watch out!"

In the evenings, Meena hurries to the beach
to watch the fishermen haul in their nets.

She splashes and swishes,
rocking boats and tangling nets.
“Slow down!” Dada says.

Meena frowns.
She digs her toes into the wet sand to stop her hurrying feet.

Meena walks calmly.
Just like Dada.

But then, her toes wiggle and her legs waggle. Meena tries to make them stop, but she doesn't know how.

SWOOSH!

Meena's feet get wild, stirring the ocean
like a tsunami. And whatever Meena does,
her hurly-burly hullabaloo does too.

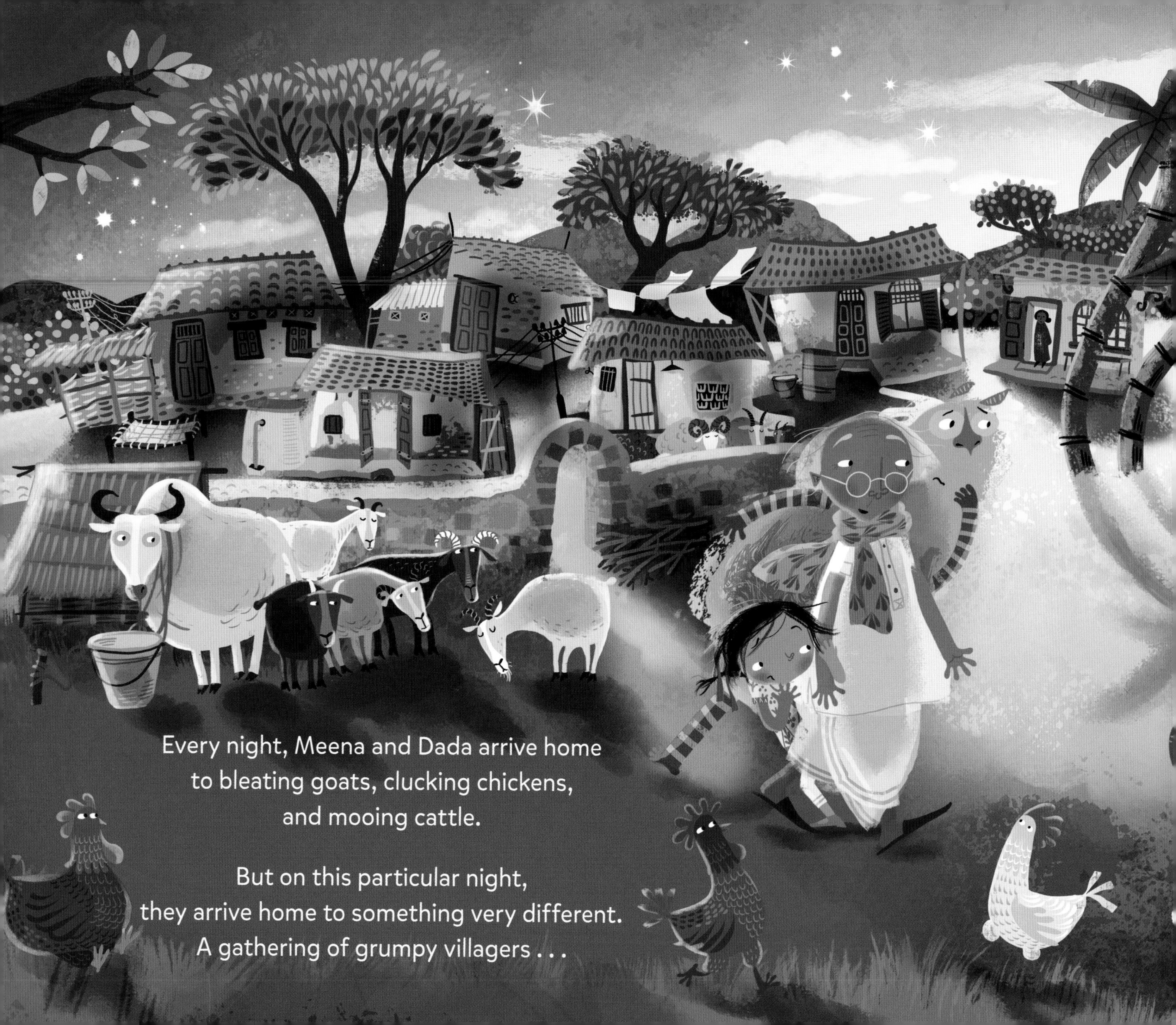

Every night, Meena and Dada arrive home
to bleating goats, clucking chickens,
and mooing cattle.

But on this particular night,
they arrive home to something very different.
A gathering of grumpy villagers . . .

rattling their carts,
wagging their fingers,
and shaking their nets.

Meena hides from the not-so-happy faces,
and Dada sends them on their way after a quiet word.

Meena feels as hazy gray as a monsoon sky. She thinks and thinks about the villagers. And the more she thinks, the worse she feels.

Dada joins Meena and they watch the sun melt into the hilltops.

Suddenly, Dada's toes start to wriggle. His legs jiggle.
"It's my hurly-burly hullabaloo," says Dada.
Meena's eyes widen. "You have one too?"

"Yes, sometimes life is just too exciting!" Dada says.
"And mine needs reminding to sit . . . to breathe . . . and to be still."

Meena's legs start to wiggle.
"Will you show me?" she asks.

"Let's try together," says Dada.

Meena takes a deep breath in . . .
. . . and then slowly blows out . . .
just like Dada.

Then she does it all over again.
And what Meena does, her hurly-burly hullabaloo does too.

The next morning, the sun shines as bright as a ripe mango. Dada and Meena set off into town. And wherever Dada and Meena go, their hurly-burly hullabaloos go too.

They walk through the park.
Dada opens his arms wide in warrior pose.
Meena breathes and tells her body to be still.

They pass shopkeepers setting up stalls.
Meena's toes wiggle and waggle, but this time she knows exactly what to do. Meena breathes and tells her feet to slow down.

They dip their toes in the cool water. Dada puts his finger to his lips. Meena breathes and tells her mind to be quiet.

Meena is calm and peaceful. And whatever Meena feels, her hurly-burly hullabaloo does too.

Dada smiles and Meena
slips her hand inside his.

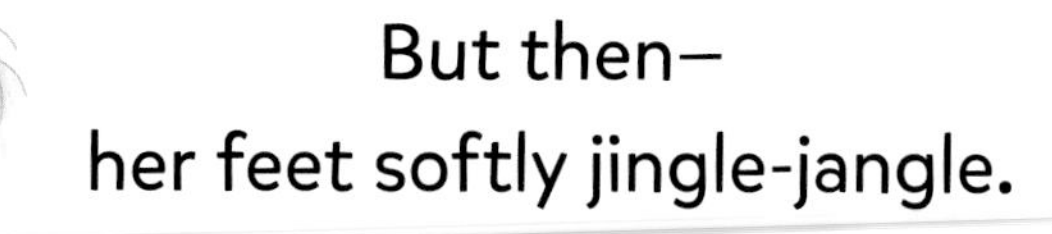

But then—
her feet softly jingle-jangle.

His toes wiggle.

"SHhHhhHHh!"